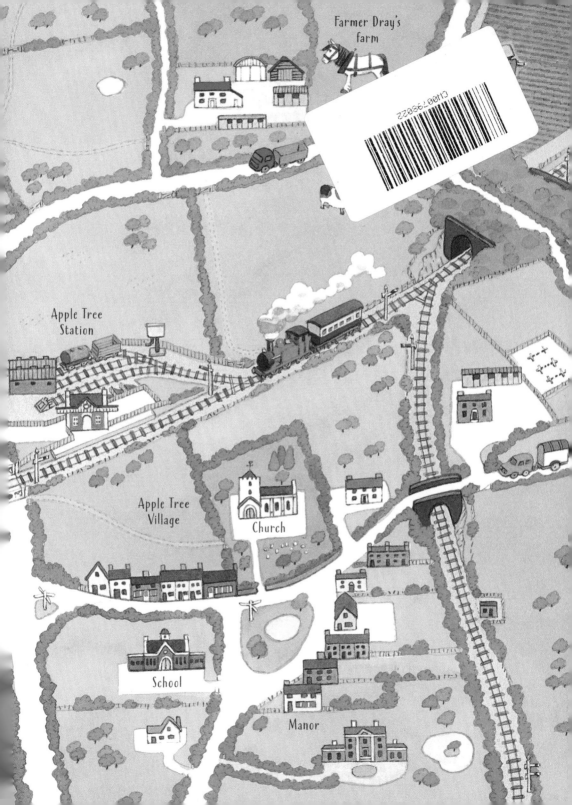

Farmer Dray's farm

Apple Tree Station

Apple Tree Village

Church

School

Manor

Usborne Farmyard Tales

Poppy and Sam's
Animal Stories

Usborne Farmyard Tales

Poppy and Sam's
Animal Stories

Based on the stories by Heather Amery
Adapted by Lesley Sims

Illustrated by Stephen Cartwright

There is a little yellow duck to find in every picture.

Contents

Welcome to Apple Tree Farm

Poppy and Sam Boot live at Apple Tree Farm. Here they are, with some of the characters you'll meet on their adventures.

Poppy   Sam   Rusty the dog   Whiskers the kitten

Mr. and Mrs. Boot   Ted, who helps on the farm

Curly the piglet

Woolly the sheep

Ears the donkey

Gertie the goat

Farmer Dray and his
carthorse, Dolly

Mr. Jones, who drives
the old steam train

Curly Gets Stuck

It was a sunny morning at Apple Tree Farm. Poppy and Sam were helping Mrs. Boot to feed the animals.

Curly, the littlest pig, was waiting
eagerly for his breakfast.

He was very hungry.

Mrs. Boot filled the trough with food. The pigs crowded around, greedily gobbling it up.

Oink! Oink!

Poor Curly! He was pushed aside and he was too little to push his way back in.

Now he was very, VERY hungry.

So he decided to go on a hunt to find
some food of his own. Carefully, he squeezed
under the fence around the pig pen.

Curly trotted across the farmyard, looking at everyone's breakfast.

Ugh!

First, he visited the cows. He didn't like the look of their breakfast, so he wandered on.

Next, he tried the sheep.

"I don't think I like hay," he thought, wrinkling his nose.

15

He even trotted all the way over to Dolly's field, to see what she was eating. Dolly was enjoying it, but it wasn't for Curly.

Curly's tummy grumbled. He was getting more and more hungry, but there was nothing he wanted to eat.

Back at Apple Tree Farm, he saw the hens' breakfast. It looked good. He sniffed. It smelled good too!

Curly spotted a gap in the fence and
s-q-u-e-e-z-e-d himself through.

OOOOOF!

The hens' breakfast tasted as good as it looked. Curly gobbled it up and licked the dish clean.

SQUAWK!

The hens were not impressed.

Just then, Mrs. Boot spotted him.

"Curly! Whatever are you doing in the hen run?" she asked.

Curly hurried back to the gap in the fence.

He tried to squeeze through... but his tummy
was too full of breakfast.

Halfway through, he got stuck.

Curly pushed and pushed. He puffed and he panted, and he pushed some more, but he couldn't move. He was completely stuck.

"Let's help him," Mrs. Boot said to Poppy and
Sam. "One, two, three... PUSH!"

They tried to be gentle, but Curly didn't like it.
He squealed loudly.

At last, with a final push, Curly popped out.
"He's free!" cried Sam.

Curly flopped forward with a grumpy grunt.

Mrs. Boot picked him up and gave him a cuddle. "There, there, all better now," she said.

Poor little pig.

"We'd better take him home," she told Poppy and Sam, and she carried him back to the pig pen.

"There you are," said Mrs. Boot, setting him down. "You can tell all the other pigs about your big adventure!"

"Don't worry," she added. "Tomorrow, I promise you will have plenty of breakfast."

And he did!

The Hungry Donkey

Ears the donkey was looking over her fence when she heard voices. She pricked up her ears...
Who was coming to visit her?

It was Poppy and Sam!

"Hello Ears, we're taking you out today," said Poppy. "We're going to a show."

"You look messy," said Sam. "I think you need to be brushed first."

Poppy brushed Ears' coat. Sam helped to harness her to a little cart.

Poppy and Sam clambered into the cart and Mrs. Boot took hold of Ears' rope. With a clippety-clop, they were off to the show.

"Giddy up, Ears!" called Sam.

At the show ground, Mrs. Boot tied Ears to a fence. "Be a good girl and wait here for us," she said. "We won't be long."

"I want to look around," said Sam. "Come on!"

Ears waited patiently for about a minute. It was boring, stuck by the fence, and she was starting to get hungry. So she pulled... and pulled... and pulled on her rope.

With one last tug, she was free.

Now, where could she find some food?
Ears sniffed the air and ambled across the
field to the show ring.

There, waiting for her, was a bright selection of flowers with some juicy-looking fruit. Yum!

Ears took a big bite of flowers and fruit, and crunched away. But they tasted horrible.

"Aaagh!" screamed Mrs. Rose. "My new hat!"

What have you done to my hat?

The scream terrified Ears and she ran, the little cart bumping along behind her.

Poppy and Sam heard the commotion and chased after Ears, followed by Mrs. Boot.

"Stop that donkey!" panted Mrs. Rose, chasing after Mrs. Boot and waving her chewed, soggy hat.

At last, Ears stopped running.
"Poor Ears, were you scared?" asked Poppy.
"You're a naughty donkey!" said Sam.

You mustn't eat hats!

"I'm so sorry about your hat," Mrs. Boot said to Mrs. Rose. "Would you like a ride in the donkey cart? I promise Ears will behave!"

Poppy and Sam helped Mrs. Rose into the
cart. Ears stood quietly. She didn't move at all.

This looks fun!

Mrs. Rose drove the cart into the show ground. Ears walked beautifully around the ring. She did exactly what Mrs. Rose told her.

Trot on, Ears!

Ears did so well that she won a prize.

"What a very well-behaved donkey," said the judge, giving Ears a ribbon.

"You win a prize too," he said to Mrs. Rose, "for such excellent driving." And he handed Mrs. Rose a brand new hat.

Hurray!

It was time to go home. "That was fun," said Poppy, as they waved goodbye to Mrs. Rose in her new hat.

Goodbye!

"Yes," said Sam. "But now I'm hungry for lunch. And I bet Ears is hungry too."

Ears smiled under her new hat. Mmm...lunch!

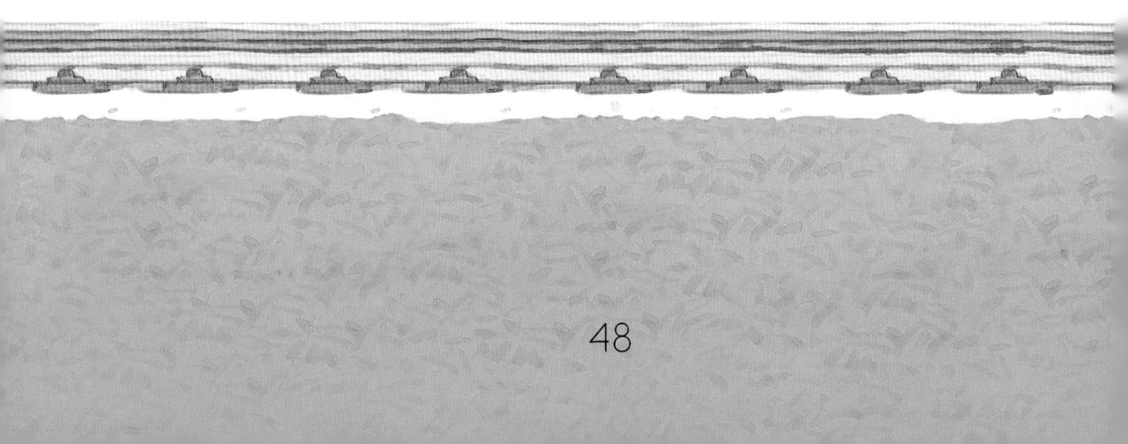

Rusty's Train Ride

Poppy and Sam were having breakfast. Rusty and Whiskers were having some breakfast too.

"What are we doing today?" asked Poppy.
"I'd like to see the steam train."
"Me too!" said Sam.

"What a good idea!" said Mrs. Boot. "Dad is helping on the train today. We'll go and say hello."

Sam held onto Rusty as they walked down the
hill to the station. Rusty stopped to watch
the rabbits.

"Hold on tight," Mrs. Boot told Sam.
"Don't let Rusty go."

At the station, the steam train pulled into the platform, billowing puffy clouds of smoke.

Poppy and Sam were waving at the train as
Mrs. Hill arrived with Mopp, her puppy.
"Ooh, I love steam trains!" she said.

Mrs. Hill went over to talk
to Mr. Jones.

"Good to see you," said Mr. Jones. "But we
can't stop now. We need to get to the next
station. Close the doors, Mr. Boot!"

"Bye, Dad!" called Sam, as Mr. Boot jumped back in the cab. "See you later."

Just then, there was a cry from Mrs. Hill. "Oh no! Where's little Mopp?"

Mopp's gone!

Rusty started pulling away from Sam.
Before Sam could stop him, Rusty had leaped
through an open train window.

Everyone watched in shock as the train
pulled away... with Rusty on board!

"Stop the train!" shouted Poppy and Sam. "STOP!" They shouted as loudly as they could, but Dad and Mr. Jones didn't hear.

Mrs. Hill was still worried about Mopp.

"Where can my little Mopp be?" she murmured.
"Don't worry," said Poppy. "I'm sure he's okay."

"What about Rusty?" Sam asked.
"We'll have to wait for the train to come back,"
said Mrs. Boot. "Rusty will be enjoying the ride."

At last, the train chugged back into the station.
A familiar face was looking out of the window.

"Rusty!" cried Poppy and Sam.
"Let's ask Dad to let him out," said Mrs. Boot.

Mr. Boot was surprised to hear about his extra passenger.
"But Mopp is still missing," said Mrs. Hill, sadly.

"Come on out, Rusty," said Mr. Boot. "Your train ride is over. What have you got there?"

Rusty trotted out, holding a little white pup.

"It's Mopp!" said Sam. "Rusty jumped on the train to look after Mopp."

Mrs. Hill scooped up Mopp. "Hello, you naughty little puppy!" she said.

Did you like your train ride?

"Isn't Rusty clever?" said Poppy. "He was the only one who saw where Mopp had gone."

"He's a very clever dog," said Mrs. Hill, with a big smile. "Thank you, Rusty!"

"He's an amazing dog sitter!" said Sam.

The Grumpy Goat

One afternoon, Poppy and Sam were helping Ted on the farm.

"We need to clean the goat shed," said Ted.

"Look at Gertie!" said Poppy. "She looks really grumpy today."

She's always grumpy!

They went into Gertie's pen so they could clean her shed. Gertie didn't like that idea at all. She butted Sam and knocked him over.

"Quick, run!" said Poppy.

Safely outside, they wondered how to get into Gertie's shed to clean it.

"I know!" said Sam. "I've had an idea."

Sam came back with a bag of bread and tried to tempt Gertie out. "Don't you want some tasty fresh bread, Gertie?" Sam asked.

Gertie ate the bread (and then the bag) but still she refused to leave the pen.

So Poppy tried. "How about some delicious grass?" she asked, tugging up handfuls and dropping them by the gate.

Gertie ate some of the grass. Then she turned around and walked away.

"This is hopeless," said Poppy.
"I've had another idea," said Sam.

"I'm going to pretend I'm Ted. Gertie likes Ted. She'll do what he says."

Sam came back in one of Ted's old hats and a baggy jacket.

Gertie wasn't fooled. She butted Sam and knocked him over again.

"Maybe we can catch her with this rope," said Poppy. "I'll try to loop it over her head."

Even Rusty tried to help but Gertie chased him...

...and they ran right out of the pen.

Quick! Shut the gate after her!

Finally, Poppy and Sam could clean out Gertie's shed. They swept out all the old straw and laid out fresh, clean straw for her instead.

"There you are, Gertie," said Sam, as soon as they were finished. "A clean, tidy home for you." Gertie grunted and went back to her field.

"How can you be grumpy with a clean shed?"
asked Sam. "Grumpy Gertie!"

The next morning, Ted came to find Poppy
and Sam. "We need to go to Gertie's shed," he said.
"But we cleaned it yesterday," said Sam.

We're
not going to
clean it!

"Oh look!" said Poppy.
"Gertie has had a baby!" said Sam.

"She has," said Ted. "No wonder she didn't want to leave her home yesterday."

Sam laughed. "She doesn't look grumpy now."

Poppy nodded. "And the baby is so sweet!"

Curly Gets Lost

"Who are we going to visit first today?" asked Poppy. She and Sam were helping to give the animals their breakfast.

"The pigs," said Mrs. Boot. "They're always ready for food!"

"Look, Rusty's found a worm!" said Sam.
"You can't be hungry, Rusty. You had some
of my toast."

When they reached the pig pen, Mrs. Boot frowned and counted the pigs. Then she counted them again.

"That's odd," she said.

There should be six pigs.

"Let's look in the vegetable garden,"
said Mrs. Boot. They looked behind the
hedge and among the baby lettuces.
Curly wasn't there.

Where can
he be?

"How about the hen run?" Mrs. Boot suggested. The hens were waiting for their breakfast. There was no sign of Curly.

95

"The cow shed," Mrs. Boot said next.

So they went to the cow shed. Poppy looked all the way around and under the trough.

Sam even looked in the trough. There was no sign of Curly anywhere.

"He might be in the barn," said Poppy.
"He is, he is, I can see him," Sam shouted.

Look, there's his tail!

But it wasn't Curly's tail at all. It was just an old piece of rope.

They were wondering where to search next
when they heard, "Woof! Woof!"

"What is the matter with Rusty?" asked
Mrs. Boot.

He's seen something!

The three of them raced over to Rusty, and there was Curly! The poor little piglet had fallen into a ditch.

Oh, good dog, Rusty!

They started to climb into the ditch. The slope was muddy and slippery.

Sam tried to be careful but his boots slipped.
He slid all the way down the bank and...

Splash! He fell into the ditch. "Oops!"

Poppy helped Sam climb out.

Mrs. Boot picked up one very muddy piglet and gave him a cuddle. "You're safe now," she said.

Sam stood up, dripping squelchy mud.

"We're all as muddy as Curly," said Poppy, with a grin.

They took Curly back to the pig pen.
The other pigs were still waiting
for their breakfast.

Curly was ready to go exploring again.
"No ditches next time!" said Mrs. Boot.

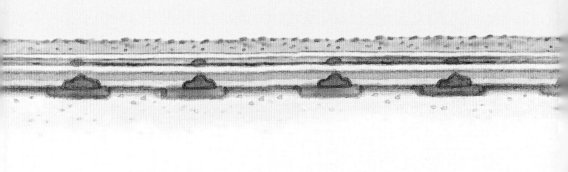

Woolly Stops
the Train

Poppy and Sam were out collecting eggs, when they heard the chug-chug-chug of Ted's tractor.

Ted looked worried.
"Is everything all right?" asked Mrs. Boot.

"I heard something while I was in the field," said Ted. "Listen..."

They all listened.

Toot! Toot!

Toot! Toot!

"Toot! Toot!" There it was again.

"That's the steam train," said Mrs. Boot.
"And it sounds as if it's in trouble."

Toot!
Toot!

Toot!
Toot!

"It's coming from over the hill," Sam said.
"Let's go and see if they need help," said Ted,
and he started to run across the field.

Rusty bounded after him and they all raced down the slope towards the train track.

"There's the train," said Poppy, pointing to a cloud of white smoke. "Why isn't it moving? Has it broken down?"

Carefully, they clambered down to the bottom of the slope. Now they could see why the train was stuck. A group of sheep was blocking the way.

Oh no!

"It's Woolly," said Mrs. Boot. "She's always escaping from her field. The other sheep must have followed her."

Sam smiled. "Maybe she wanted the sheep to have a day out," he said.

"That's all very well," said Mrs. Boot, "but it's time for them to come home... We'll all have to herd them back. But first, we need to get them off the track."

They went up to the sheep.

"Shoo! Shoo!" said Mrs. Boot, waving her arms and pointing to the grass at the side of the track. The sheep jostled each other a little, but they stayed where they were.

"Come on, MOVE!" said Ted, in a firm voice, striding behind them. Poppy, Sam and Mrs. Boot joined in, calling "Shoo!"

At last, the sheep started to move, though Rusty had to persuade Woolly. "But how will we get them up the slope to go home?" wondered Mrs. Boot.

119

"I know," said Sam. "Let's put them on the train!"
"That's a brilliant idea," said Mrs. Boot.

Poppy and Sam herded the sheep to the front
of the train, where Ted lifted them up to Mrs. Boot.
"Oof! They've eaten a lot of grass," he panted.

"Thanks for your help!" said Mr. Jones.
"I thought I would be stuck for ages."

"You're going on a train," Poppy said to Woolly.
"All aboard!"

Poppy and Sam scrambled onto the train, with Rusty and Ted close behind.

"We're ready to go," Mrs. Boot called. "Thank you, Mr. Jones!"

Mr. Jones took off the brake and the train started to move, slowly at first, but then picking up speed.

Poppy and Sam pressed their faces to the windows, as the train puffed through the countryside.

Finally, they reached Apple Tree Station.
"I was getting worried," said the station master.
"What kept you?"

He had a shock when he saw the passengers
get off the train.

"I'm afraid we don't have tickets," said Mrs. Boot.
"Today's baaaaa-rgain day!" said Ted.

After their train ride, the sheep were happy to be herded home. Sam, Mrs. Boot and Rusty led the way. Poppy and Ted followed after the sheep, making sure none were left behind.

"That was an adventure!" said Sam. He laughed. "What will naughty Woolly get up to next?"

The Silly Sheepdog

Poppy, Sam and Rusty were helping Mrs. Boot to pick up sticks for firewood. Just then, there came a...

Beep! Beep!

Ted pulled up in his blue truck. "I've bought a sheepdog to help with the sheep!" he said.

"Hello Patch!" said Sam.

"Welcome to Apple Tree Farm," said Poppy.
"Come on, we'll show you around."

First, they visited the hens. But Patch jumped into the pen and started chasing them.

The frightened hens squawked in shock and flew up to the roof of the hen house.

"You silly dog," said Sam.

Next, they went to see the cows. Patch ran amongst the cows and started barking at them, too. The cows just stared.

"Those are cows, Patch," said Poppy.

"Let's take him to see the pigs," said Sam.
Patch jumped into the pig pen and chased all
the pigs into the sty.

"Patch! What are you doing?" cried Poppy.

Sam scolded Patch. "You're a very silly sheepdog," he said. "You're supposed to chase sheep, not hens or cows or pigs."

"I think Ted will have to send him back," said Poppy. "He's the silliest sheepdog I've ever seen."

They decided to show Patch the sheep. Ted was by the fence, looking worried.

"Why are there only five sheep?" Poppy asked. "There should be six."

"I know," said Ted. "It's that naughty Woolly. She's gone missing. Again."

Suddenly, Patch barked and ran off.

"Where's he going?" said Ted.

Poppy, Sam, Ted and Rusty all raced across the field after Patch.

Patch had run to a boy and jumped up at him, barking happily.

Hello, Patch! How are you?

"Hello," the boy said, as Poppy, Sam and Ted caught up with Patch. "I found this sheep on the road. Is she yours?"

"Yes, that's Woolly," smiled Poppy.

"How do you know Patch?" Sam asked the boy.

"He used to live on my parents' farm," the boy explained. "He's a good sheepdog."

"He's not," said Sam. "He's a silly sheepdog."
"Watch," said the boy. He put two fingers
in his mouth and gave a loud whistle.

Patch chased Woolly through the gate and back
into the field with the other sheep.

"Goodness me!" said Ted. "I can't get him to do anything I tell him."

"You just need to whistle," said the boy. "I can teach you if you like."

"That would be great, thank you!" said Ted,
as Patch ran back to them.

"Maybe he can teach me to whistle too," thought Poppy.

"You're not a silly sheepdog after all," said Sam.

Sorry, Patch!

148

The New Pony

Poppy and Sam were out for a walk with their dad and Rusty. They wandered down the lane and past a field belonging to Old Gate Farm.

"Look, there's a pony!" said Poppy.
"That must be Mr. Stone's pony," Mr. Boot
told them. "He's just bought the farm."

The pony looked sad. Her coat was rough and dirty and her mane was tangled.

Rusty ran up to say hello, but the pony didn't even look up.

Poppy tried to pat her nose and the pony backed away.

"Be careful," Mr. Boot warned her. "Mr. Stone said she sometimes has a bad temper."

"She's just shy," said Poppy. "And I think she looks hungry."

The next day, Poppy went back to the field with a bag full of apples. She held out an apple to the pony, keeping her hand flat and still.

"Try this," she said gently.

The pony sniffed at the apple and took a bite.
Soon, she was crunching up every apple in the bag.

The day after that, Sam came too. But the pony was gone. The field was empty, apart from a curious rabbit who popped his head out of his burrow to watch them.

156

"I think we should look for her," said Poppy, and she opened the gate.

Rusty bounded into the field. Sam wasn't so sure. He felt a little scared.

"She may need us," said Poppy, going through.

At the top of the field, Sam stopped. "I can see her!" he called. "Look, she's stuck down by the hedge."

The pony was caught on a broken fence.

Poppy and Sam rushed back to Apple Tree Farm.

"Dad, the pony," shouted Sam. "She's stuck and she might be hurt!"

Please come quickly!

Mr. Boot ran back to the field with Poppy and Sam. Gently, he walked up to the pony.

"She's caught her harness," he said quietly, unhooking it from the fence.

That's better.

The pony wasn't hurt at all.

"You're safe now," said Poppy, stroking the pony on her velvety nose.

"Hey, you girl!" came a sudden, angry shout. "Get away from my pony."

It was Mr. Stone and he looked furious.

"We were only trying to help," said Poppy.

Mr. Stone didn't want to hear their explanation.

"Please take care of your pony," Poppy begged Mr. Stone. He turned red in the face.

"How dare you..." he began.

"Come on, Poppy," said Mr. Boot, quickly. "The pony is fine now. Let's go home."

The next morning, there was a surprise for Poppy and Sam.

It was the pony! She was a present for Poppy from Mr. Stone.

"He was sorry he was angry," said Mr. Boot.

"I'm going to call her Penny Pippin," said Poppy.
"Pippin for short."

"Welcome to Apple Tree Farm, Pippin!" said Sam.

Naughty Woolly!

"Eat up!" said Mrs. Boot, one morning. "We're off to the country fair today."

"Hurray!" said Sam. "What's that?"

"People show things from their farms,"
said Mrs. Boot. "They show the things
they grow and sometimes their animals."

Let's show them
our apples.

After breakfast, they went to the apple tree. It was full of ripe shiny apples. Soon, they had picked enough for two baskets.

We could take some flowers too.

They were so busy talking about the fair that they didn't notice the open gate...

...but Woolly did.

"I wonder what's outside this field," thought
Woolly. She looked around.

The other sheep were munching grass. So she walked to the open gate and dashed through.

She wandered along until she found another open gate. This one led to a wonderful garden.

The flowers looked beautiful...

...and they tasted delicious! Woolly ate her way through them all, yellow ones, red ones, blue ones, pink ones, purple ones and, finally, orange ones.

Yum, yum!

Just then, Rusty noticed Woolly in the garden and started barking.

"Woolly!" shouted Mrs. Boot, when she saw the state of the garden. "What have you done?"

She was very upset. "The flowers are ruined," she said. "I can't take any to the fair now."

You naughty sheep!

"Don't be sad," said Poppy. "We have the apples and they're perfect."

Mrs. Boot was still thinking about her flowers.
Sam was impatient to get to the fair.

So Mrs. Boot found their coats and they set off.

Woolly watched them go.

She decided to visit the fair too.

Woolly trotted all the way there. Then she trotted through the entrance. There were lots of people, all eager to visit the fair. No one noticed Woolly joining them.

Woolly saw some other sheep and went over.
"Well, well, who do we have here?" said a man
in a long white coat and a hat.

"Baaaa!" said Woolly.

"Not again!" said a voice.

Mrs. Boot had just seen Woolly. "What mischief are you up to now?"

184

The man in the white coat smiled. "Your sheep has just won the first prize in the best sheep competition!"

"Clever Woolly," said Sam, as they all headed home.

"Naughty Woolly for eating my flowers," said Mrs. Boot.

She smiled at the cup. "But I'm not sure my flowers would have won a cup," she added.

"Clever, naughty Woolly!"

Dolly and the Train

Poppy and Sam were buzzing with
excitement. Today was the day of
the school picnic.

"Come on, Poppy!" called Mrs. Boot.
"Bring Rusty if you like. He can walk
with us to the old station."

At the station, all their friends and their teacher, Miss Smith, had gathered on the platform.

Lovely day for a picnic!

The steam train was already puffing out smoke, its engine gleaming in the sun.

"All aboard," cried the station master, who was going on the outing too. "Don't forget your picnics."

"Watch your step!" said Miss Smith.

With a "Choo! Choo!" the train puffed out of the station. Mrs. Boot waved until it was almost out of sight.

Rusty barked after them. He wanted to go on a picnic too.

For a while, the train clickety-clacked along the track. Then, all of a sudden, it stopped.

Everyone looked out of the window.
"Are there sheep on the track?" asked Sam.

195

Miss Smith leaned out of the window.

"The engine has broken down," shouted Jim, who was helping Mr. Jones for the day.

"Don't worry," Mr. Jones added. "The station master is going for help."

Jim brought a ladder to the train so everyone could climb out.

"We can have our picnic here," Miss Smith told them.

"Let's go into the field," said Sam. "That's a good place for a picnic." They had just started climbing over the fence when...

"STOP!" shouted Miss Smith. "There's a bull in that field!"

Poppy laughed. "That's not a bull, Miss Smith. That's Buttercup."

She's a friendly cow.

"Oh," said Miss Smith. "Well, it's time for the picnic, so everyone sit down over here."

Soon the only sounds were the snapping open
of lunch boxes and contented munching.
"Hullo there!" someone called.

Farmer Dray was coming over the field,
leading his carthorse, Dolly.

"He has the station master with him," said Sam.
"He must have asked Farmer Dray for help."

"How is a horse going to help us?" said Miss
Smith. "Dolly can't give us all a ride home!"

They watched as Farmer Dray led Dolly alongside the train track.

Mr. Jones guessed what Farmer Dray was going to do. "I'll unhitch the engine," he said.

202

"Everyone back on board," said Miss Smith,
as Farmer Dray tied Dolly to the back of the train.

"Ready when you are," Farmer Dray
called out.

With everyone on board, Farmer Dray patted
Dolly. "Let's go," he said, and Dolly started to pull.

Slowly, very slowly, they began to move along the track.

"Clever Dolly, pulling all of us!" said Sam.

Mrs. Boot was very surprised to see a horse-drawn train pull into the station.

"The engine broke down," Poppy told her. "But Farmer Dray and Dolly saved the day!"

"They did indeed," agreed Miss Smith. "But I'm sorry the outing was ruined."

"It wasn't ruined. It was an adventure!" said Sam. "I think it was the best outing ever."

Cover illustration by Simon Taylor-Kielty
Edited by Jane Chisholm

Designed by Karen Tomlins, Marc Maynard, Krysia Ellis,
Kate Rimmer and Reuben Barrance

Digital manipulation: Keith Furnival

First published in 2019 by Usborne Publishing Ltd.,
Usborne House, 83-85 Saffron Hill, London EC1N 8RT, England.
www.usborne.com Copyright © 2019, 2016, 2015, 1989-1996 Usborne Publishing Ltd.

Camping

Ted's
house

Apple Tree
Farm

Apple Tree
Brook

Old
Mill